Margaret Peterson Haddix

DEXTER
THE
TOUGH

Illustrated by Mark Elliott

Simon & Schuster Books for Young Readers
New York London Toronto Sydney

For Hugh Morgan

Acknowledgments

With thanks to two great teachers, Janet Terrell and Kristi Jerger, for answering my "What if . . . ?" questions. I also greatly appreciate the help from my friends Dr. Andy Schuster and Dr. Dara Schuster, and— from the Arthur G. James Cancer Hospital and Richard J. Solove Research Institute at the Ohio State University—Jan Sirilla, administrative director of the blood and marrow transplant program, and Eileen Scahill, media relations program manager, who filled in the gaps in my medical knowledge and suggested a few "What if . . . ?'s" of their own.

SIMON & SCHUSTER BOOKS FOR YOUNG READERS
An imprint of Simon & Schuster Children's Publishing Division
1230 Avenue of the Americas, New York, New York 10020
Book design by Einav Aviram
The text for this book is set in Hadriano.
The illustrations for this book are rendered in pencil.
Manufactured in the United States of America
2 4 6 8 10 9 7 5 3 1
Library of Congress Cataloging-in-Publication Data
Haddix, Margaret Peterson.
Dexter the tough / Margaret Peterson Haddix. — 1st ed.
p. cm.
Summary: A sympathetic teacher and her writing assignment help fourth-grader Dexter deal with being the new kid in school after he punches a kid on the first day.
ISBN-13: 978-1-4169-1159-3
ISBN-10: 1-4169-1159-6
[1. Friendship—Fiction. 2. Authorship—Fiction. 3. Schools—Fiction.] I. Title.
PZ7.H1164Dex 2007
[Fic]—dc22
2006009403

FIRST
F
EDITION

Chapter 1

Dexter hated his new school already.

It was only his first day—barely his first hour. So far Dexter had decided that he hated the principal, the school secretary, and the janitor. He hadn't even met the janitor yet, but he hated him anyway. The janitor had made the floor so shiny and slick that Dexter slipped on it, falling right in front of a bunch of other kids.

Dexter hated those kids, too. They laughed at him.

Now he was standing in front of his new fourth-grade class, a sea of staring eyes.

"Dexter moved here from Cincinnati,"

his new teacher said. "Dexter, would you like to tell us a little about yourself?"

"No," Dexter said.

The smile on his teacher's face didn't shrink at all.

"Well, that's quite all right, Dexter," she said in a fake, cheerful voice. "I know it can be kind of scary being new."

Dexter wanted to say, *Oh, no, I'm not scared. Not me.* But the teacher was already showing him to his desk. Her too-wide smile stretched back almost to her ears.

"It's so *wonderful* that you've joined us today, Dexter, because we're starting on the *most* exciting writing project," she said as Dexter slipped into his seat.

She was wearing huge star earrings that seemed to twinkle at the class. He could tell already: She was going to be one of those sparkly, enthusiastic teachers.

He hated that kind of teacher.

"Don't you all want to hear what the project is?" the teacher asked.

"Yes, Ms. Abbott," the whole class except Dexter chorused together.

Disgusting. The other kids were going to be as sparkly and enthusiastic as the teacher.

"Great!" the teacher said. "We're going to be working on the same piece of writing every day for a *month*! We're going to pretend we're all professional writers, and that's how they work. They don't just write something and say, 'Hurray! I'm done! Isn't this wonderful?' They write a story and then they go back and rewrite it, and revise it, and make it as good as possible. Some writers may rewrite the same story dozens of times! What do you think of that?"

Dexter thought that professional writers must be pretty stupid. He wondered if he should add professional writers to the list of people he hated.

"We'll start out today just writing the first draft," the teacher said, still all twinkly and cheerful. "Get out a piece of paper and tell me a story. It can be a true story or it can be made up. But"—her eyes seemed to rest on Dexter for a moment—"I'd really like it if you could tell me a story that lets me know more about who you are!"

All the other kids started writing right away. Dexter sat frozen at his desk.

"Dexter?" the teacher said. "Don't you have pencil and paper?"

Staring down at his empty desktop, Dexter shook his head. No. He didn't have anything he needed.

"That's okay," the teacher said, slipping a pencil into his hand and sliding paper onto his desk. "I'll send a note home with you tonight to let your parents know what school supplies to buy."

Dexter clutched the pencil so hard he was surprised it didn't snap in two.

"It's my grandmother," he blurted.

"Excuse me?" the teacher said, and for the first time, she didn't look sparkly or twinkly. She looked confused.

"You have to send the note to my grandmother, not my parents," Dexter said, the words coming out in a rush. "I live with her now."

"All right," the teacher said. "No problem. Let's get started writing, okay?"

Maybe it was no problem for her, but now there was a huge lump in Dexter's throat, which made it hard for him to swallow. It kind of made it hard for him to breathe. He stared down at the blank sheet of paper on his desk. Every other kid in the class was writing like crazy. He could hear the pencils racing. He saw one girl already flipping over her sheet of paper, to start on her second page. Dexter couldn't even remember exactly what he was supposed to be writing. Something about letting the teacher know who he was. Fine. He could do that.

He gripped the pencil and printed:

I'm the new kid. I am tuf.

He put the pencil down.

"Some of you who finish early might want to start your revision process now," the teacher said from the front of the room. "Add details, descriptions, examples!"

Examples.

Dexter picked up his pencil again. His hand shook a little as he wrote:

This morning I beat up a kid.

It was kind of scary seeing those words in black and white. He stared down at his paper, and the words seemed to stare back at him. He put his hands over the paper so all he could see was one sentence: "I am tuf."

I am, he told himself. *I am. So there.*

"All right, everyone," the teacher said. "Make sure your names are on your papers and hand them in. Even if you aren't done, Marleeza."

A girl in the front, who'd started waving one hand in the air, abruptly put her arm back down.

Someone behind Dexter poked him in the shoulder and handed him a stack of papers. Dexter stuffed his own paper in the middle of the stack, so no one would see it. Then he handed the whole stack to the kid in front of him.

Dexter's stomach churned as he watched the teacher's hands gather all the papers together. Her long fingers smoothed the ragged edges, making the pile neat.

"I'm so excited to start reading these!" the teacher said. "It's almost time for recess anyhow. I'll let you go a few minutes early, to reward you for all your hard work. And when you return, we'll begin workshopping!"

Why did I write that? Dexter wondered. *Why?*

His hands itched to grab his paper back before the teacher saw it. But how could he do that? What would he tell her?

The paper was lost to him now. The teacher was holding all the papers too tightly.

He squared his shoulders. He tried to ignore the sick twisting in his stomach.

Who cares? he told himself.

He walked out of the room behind the other kids. He didn't let himself look back.

Chapter 2

Dexter spent the whole recess huddled by the side of the building, alone. Once a boy came over and asked, "Want to play kickball with us?" Dexter just shook his head. His throat felt too swollen to let out the word, "No."

He dug the toe of his tennis shoe into the pebbles that covered the ground between the building and the grass. He lifted his foot a little. Some of the pebbles skipped over the tops of the others. Some of them hit the side of the school.

Dexter slid his foot through the pebbles again, scattering more of them. It felt really good to kick something. Dexter liked the sound the little stones made, hitting the school. It was the first thing he'd liked all day.

"Stop that!" a woman Dexter hadn't noticed yelled at him. "Are you trying to break a window?"

Dexter wasn't anywhere near a window. He turned his back and walked away from the woman without answering.

At his old school he would have said, "Sorry." No—at his old school he wouldn't have been standing around kicking pebbles. He would have been out playing with his friends. Jaydell and Dillon and Robert and C. J. They didn't play sissy games like kickball. They played football and basketball. They . . .

Don't think about it, he told himself.

The woman who'd yelled at Dexter blew a whistle. Dexter guessed that meant that recess was over, because all the other kids came running over, laughing as they got into lines. Dexter wasn't sure which line to get into. He hadn't looked very closely at any of the other kids in his class.

Oh, wait. That girl with the big red bow in her hair—wasn't she the one who'd raised her hand when the teacher said to stop writing?

Dexter stepped into line behind her, almost letting himself feel glad that he'd remembered the red bow. But they were marching back to class now, marching back to the teacher who'd probably read his paper by now.

"Dexter? Would you like to go first?" the teacher said, as soon as they were settled in their desks again, as soon as she'd explained that everyone else was going to have silent reading time while she "workshopped" with each student.

No, Dexter didn't want to go first. He didn't even want to be there. He wanted to be back home in Cincinnati, at his old school, where he belonged. Where he would be right this minute, playing basketball at recess with his friends, if only—

"Dexter?" the teacher said again, motioning him toward her desk.

Somehow Dexter's feet carried him to the front of the room. His heart thudded so loudly he couldn't quite hear what she was telling him to do. Oh. Sit down. All he had to do was sit down. He slid into a smaller chair beside the teacher's desk. She bent her head down over his paper, reading what he'd written.

She frowned.

"Oh, dear," she said. "Beating someone up . . . A fight . . . This isn't true, is it, Dexter? You didn't hurt another child, did you?"

She peered at him across the desk. She had blue eyes. Dexter hadn't noticed that before. Her eyes were the color of the sky on a beautiful spring day, the color of a marble Dexter's dad had given him once, explaining that it'd been his when he was a little boy. "When kids actually still played marbles," Dad had said with a laugh, flexing his muscles dramatically and surprising Dexter by flicking the marble clear across the room.

That had been when Dad actually still had muscles.

"Dexter?" the teacher said gently.

Dexter felt his face get hot. Beating up a kid was fighting. And of course, fighting would be a very bad thing at this school, just as it had been at his old school. Only bad kids got in fights.

Maybe I am a bad kid now, Dexter thought.

The teacher's blue eyes were begging him to say it wasn't true, he hadn't really been in a fight.

Bad kids don't just get in fights, Dexter thought. *They lie, too. If I'm a bad kid, I can do anything I want.*

"No," Dexter said. "It isn't true."

He was surprised at how strong his voice sounded, how easy it was to lie.

The teacher leaned back in her chair.

"I'm very glad to hear that," she said, smiling again, the twinkle back in her voice. "Not that I really believed that you'd beat someone up . . . ."

The way she was looking at him made Dexter's face feel even hotter.

Oh, yeah? he wanted to say. *You think I'm too small to win a fight? Too scrawny to beat anyone up?*

People were always talking about how tiny Dexter was. He'd weighed just four pounds when he was born, so he'd started out behind. The only big thing about him was his eyes, which always seemed to take up half his face in pictures.

"Just tell people that one of these days, you *are* going to grow into those eyes of yours," Dexter's mom used to say sometimes. "And then—watch out!"

That was back when Dexter's mom had time to say anything about Dexter. When she had time to be his mom.

Dexter swallowed hard. He lifted his arm, which seemed to be shaking a little, and pointed to one sentence on his paper:

I am tuf.

He wasn't sure if he was reminding himself or the teacher.

The teacher looked a little bit confused. Then she laughed. As far as Dexter was concerned, this teacher laughed way too much.

"Oh, very good, Dexter," she said. "You noticed that you spelled a word wrong! This is what's so great about revision, when you can find your own mistakes and fix them. We don't usually worry too much about spelling until the last stages of revision, but since you saw it already—what should you have written instead of 't-u-f'?"

Dexter shrugged. This teacher didn't understand at all.

"It's t-o-u-g-h," the teacher said, writing it in big letters at the top of his paper.

That seemed wrong, too. "T-o-u-g-h" didn't look tough at all.

"But I was thinking . . . ," the teacher went on. "It's not really . . . appropriate for you to write about a fight. Especially since you didn't really beat someone up. Thank goodness!" She was smiling again, and waiting for Dexter to say something.

Dexter just looked at her.

"It would really be better for you to write about a different topic," she said, trying again. "Can you think of anything else you want to write about?"

Dexter knew what he was supposed to do. He was supposed to agree. He was supposed to crumple up his paper with the misspelled "t-u-f" and the guilty sentence, "This morning I beat up a kid." He was supposed to start over again and write about something nice, like flowers or butterflies or how happy he was to be at his new school. Just like he was supposed to help Grandma and not be any trouble. Just like he was supposed to tell Mom or Dad on the phone every night that everything was going great and he didn't mind at all being sent away.

"No," Dexter said.

The word didn't come out sounding t-u-f, or t-o-u-g-h. It just sounded sad. But the teacher looked at him carefully, for a long time.

"Okay, then," she finally said. "Let's think about revising. You need to give more information, to tell the whole story. Where did this fight happen? Why would you beat up this other boy—it is a boy, isn't it? What's his name? Everybody has a name. Names are very important. In a story you have to let your readers know who your characters are."

She wrote her three questions on Dexter's paper, each of her letters perfectly shaped, each of her words perfectly spaced.

"That's what you can work on for tomorrow," she said. She seemed to be trying to smile again, but her eyes didn't twinkle like they had before.

Dexter walked back to his seat, the paper clutched in his hand. His legs trembled like he'd been in another fight.

This time he didn't know if he'd won or lost.

Chapter 3

It was true, of course. Dexter had beaten up a kid.

That morning, after he'd gotten mad at the school principal, and the school secretary, and the janitor, and the kids who laughed at him, Dexter had walked into the bathroom. A boy was standing at the sink. And Dexter punched him.

How am I supposed to know what his name was? Dexter wondered, slumped in his desk again. *It's not like I asked him.*

Dexter looked around the classroom, just in case the kid from the bathroom was in his class. All the other kids had their heads bent dutifully over their books, reading silently. Just like they were supposed to. The boy in the bathroom had looked like the kind of kid who would do what he was supposed to. But none of Dexter's classmates looked like the kid Dexter had hit.

Later, at lunchtime, Dexter looked around the school cafeteria. He looked around the playground at the next recess.

What if I hurt that kid so bad he had to go home? What if he was gushing blood and they had to take him to the emergency room? What if he died?

Dexter started to get scared again. He started thinking about the police coming and arresting him. He started thinking about Mom and Dad and Grandma all crying as Dexter was led away in handcuffs. No—just Grandma, because Mom and Dad wouldn't be there. They were thousands of miles away, not even in Cincinnati anymore, not even on the same side of the country. Mom had shown him on a map. "Here's Cincinnati, here's Bellgap, Kentucky, where Grandma lives, here's where we'll be at the hospital in Seattle. . . ." But Dexter's eyes had blurred looking at the map, all the bright colors of the different states blending together. Even now, thinking about it, he started having to blink a lot because the wind was making his eyes water.

That was when he saw the boy he'd hit.

The boy was sitting by himself under a tree, far away from the kickball game, and the girls playing hopscotch, and the little kids on the swings and slides. He was picking blades of grass and peeling them apart and throwing them back on the ground. Was it really the right kid? The main thing Dexter remembered about the boy in the bathroom was the way he had such neat, careful comb tracks in his blond hair. The boy under the tree had blond hair, all right, but the wind was blowing it all around. It was a mess.

Dexter walked toward the boy. He stopped and leaned against the tree trunk.

"Hey," Dexter said from behind.

The boy jumped a little, like he was surprised. Then he turned around and saw Dexter, and his face scrunched up in fear. He started to scramble to his feet, like he wanted to run away.

Like he was scared of Dexter.

"It's okay," Dexter said. "I'm not going to hurt you. I promise. I just want to ask you a question."

"What?" the boy whispered, still crouching, half-up, half-down.

"What's your name?"

"R—" The boy had to clear his throat. "Robin," he said in a shaky voice.

Robin? Dexter thought. *Robin?* He'd been thinking of this boy as someone who had a mom who took really, really good care of him. Because of the comb tracks. But what kind of mean, nasty parents would name their son after a bird?

"Go ahead and make fun of it," Robin said bitterly. "Everyone else does. 'Want to eat a worm, Robin?' 'Aren't you flying south for the winter, Robin?'"

Back home, Dexter's friends sometimes made jokes about Dexter's name—"Where's your laboratory, Dexter?"—because of the TV show. Sometimes the jokes were even funny. But Dexter always thought his name was cool, because it was the same as his dad's middle name. It'd be awful to be named something like "Robin." *He* wasn't going to make fun of it.

Dexter shrugged and started to turn away. Then he thought of something else.

"What's your last name?" he asked.

The way his teacher acted about writing, she'd probably insist on full names in Dexter's story.

"Bryce," Robin said.

"That's a good name," Dexter said, because he was starting to feel a little bit sorry that he'd beaten up Robin, if Robin already had people making fun of him all the time. And Robin was still half up and half down, looking

at Dexter like he still thought Dexter was going to hit him again, right in front of the playground monitor and everyone.

"If I was you," Dexter offered, "I think I'd just have people call me by my last name. Just say, 'Hi, I'm Bryce.' And then nobody would even know that your real name was Robin."

"Everybody already knows me," Robin said sulkily. But he sat back down a little, not so ready to run.

"*I* didn't," Dexter said. "I'm new. You could have just told me to call you Bryce and I never would have known any different."

Robin squinted up at Dexter.

"My middle name's William," he finally said. "That's better, isn't it?"

"Yeah," Dexter said. "You could be 'Bill' or 'Billy' or something like that."

Robin stared off into the distance.

"No," he said after a while. "I really like being Robin. I just don't like other kids making fun of it. Maybe . . ." He looked sideways at Dexter. "Maybe I could tell them you'll beat them up if they keep doing that?"

Dexter's stomach started feeling funny again.

"Beat them up yourself," Dexter said.

"I'm not very good at fighting," Robin said, shrugging helplessly. "You saw me this morning."

Dexter had a flash of remembering his fist hitting Robin's jaw. He felt like he was going to throw up that weird tuna fish sandwich Grandma had packed for his lunch.

"Look," Dexter said. "You're a lot bigger than me. Stand up."

Obediently, Robin scrambled all the way up. Dexter's nose barely came up to the middle of Robin's chest.

"Let me see your muscles."

Robin lifted his arm, and bent it at the elbow. Maybe he had more flab than muscle, but his arm was at least twice as thick as Dexter's.

"See, if you'd really tried, you could have

beaten *me* up," Dexter said encouragingly. "If you'd gotten one good hit in, you would have knocked me out. You probably would have put me in the hospital."

"Yeah?" Robin said excitedly.

"Oh, yeah," Dexter said, nodding. "I'm sure of it. So just tell the other kids *that*."

Robin let his arm fall to his side.

"My mom would kill me if she heard I was telling people stuff like that," he said hopelessly. "Even if I said you would beat them up. She doesn't approve of fighting. She's really picky like that."

Dexter felt his fists clench together. And if the playground monitor hadn't blown her whistle just then, ending recess, he might have beaten Robin up all over again.

No matter what he'd promised.

Chapter 4

Grandma was waiting at the curb when Dexter got off the bus that afternoon. She had curly white old-lady hair, and sturdy brown old-lady shoes, and a stretchy red old-lady pantsuit. Dexter hoped nobody on the bus thought she was his mom.

"You don't have to come and get me," he said, first thing, as soon as he stepped off the bus.

Grandma gave him a tired smile.

"I know," she said. "I know you're a big boy. But I thought it might feel a little strange to you, coming home to a different house." She pushed open the gate that separated her yard from the sidewalk. "How was your first day of school?"

Dexter thought about how much he hated the principal, and the secretary, and the janitor, and his teacher, and the kids who had laughed at him. He thought about how he'd gotten in a fight—how he'd beaten up Robin Bryce.

Then he thought about how Mom and Dad had said he wasn't supposed to make any trouble for Grandma, how he wasn't supposed to worry her.

"It was okay," he said. "The teacher sent home a list of supplies I need." He pulled the sheet of paper out of his backpack and handed it to Grandma.

Grandma frowned.

"Oh, dear," she said. "Back when your mother and Uncle Ted were in school, kids just needed paper and something to write with. What's this—colored pencils? Fat markers and skinny ones, too?" She sighed. "Guess we'll have to run out to the store after dinner."

"I have markers at home," Dexter said. "I just forgot to bring them."

Why hadn't Mom or Dad reminded him? Dexter felt mad again. He kicked at the step as he climbed toward Grandma's porch. But his kick missed and he lost his balance and fell over backward. He landed flat on the sidewalk. He thought he heard kids laughing as the bus pulled away.

Grandma squinted down at him.

Mom would have said, "Child, just *what* do you think you're doing?" And Dad would have said, "A swing—and a miss! Strike one! Can we see the instant replay? Bet you couldn't do that again if you tried!" But Grandma said in a scared voice, "Are you all right?" And somehow that made Dexter feel worse, like maybe there was something really, really wrong with him. Had Dad's problems started with him falling down?

"I'm fine," Dexter told Grandma fiercely, as he jumped back up. His ankle hurt now, and he'd banged his elbow hard. He tried not to limp across the porch.

Grandma still looked worried.

"I made you a snack," she said, pushing open the front door. "I remember how your mom and Uncle Ted were always so hungry, getting home from school. Just come on into the kitchen."

The snack was graham crackers and canned pears. Dexter looked down at the pears in their slimy syrup and felt his throat starting to close over again.

"Do you have any homework?" Grandma said, sliding into the chair across from him. "Anything you need help with?"

"Uh, no," Dexter said. "I mean, yes, I have some homework. But I don't need help."

Grandma just sat there.

"I can do it by myself," Dexter repeated. He really, really, really didn't want Grandma to see the story he'd written, the one he had to rewrite.

"Okay," Grandma said, inching her chair back. She clutched the table, and pulled herself up. "I'll leave you to it, then. I'll be in the living room watching TV if you need me." She began to hobble away.

Dexter waited until she was gone. He heard her heaving herself onto the living room couch. He listened for the TV to come on before he pulled his story out of his backpack. He smoothed it out on the table. He drew a big *X* through everything he'd written before. Then he put the point of his pencil down directly beneath his teacher's questions:

I'm the new kid, he wrote. He started to write, I am tuf again, but it wasn't worth it if he had to spell the word "t-o-u-g-h."

This morning I beat up Robin Bryce. In the bathroom. The one between the office and your classroom. With the blue tile on the wall.

He looked at the teacher's questions again. He'd answered everything except "Why did you get in a fight?" He took a break and spooned one of the slimy pear slices up to his mouth. It slithered down his throat like some tiny animal, a fish or a toad or a lizard. It seemed to be fighting to come back up. Dexter swallowed hard. He chewed a graham cracker that tasted soggy and nasty and old. Maybe it came out of a box that Grandma had kept from when Mom and Uncle Ted were little. Maybe one of them had cried on it. It tasted like tears.

He pressed his pencil down hard against his paper.

I was mad, he wrote.

Chapter 5

Dexter put his story back in his backpack. He put the rest of the canned pears in the garbage. He put the box of graham crackers on the counter. He stood in the middle of the kitchen floor wondering what he was supposed to do next.

"Ha-ha-ha-ha-ha!"

Someone on Grandma's TV show was laughing.

Dexter tiptoed into the living room. On the TV screen a little girl was standing in front of a whole classroom of other kids, and they were all laughing at her because her mother had used the wrong laundry detergent. Dexter had seen this commercial before. He used to laugh at it himself. Now he looked over at the couch to see if Grandma was laughing too.

Grandma had her head tilted back and her eyes closed. Her glasses were practically falling off the tip of her nose. Her mouth hung open, her chin sagging down toward her chest. She wasn't moving. It didn't even look like she was breathing.

Oh, no. What if Grandma was dead?

"Grandma?" Dexter whispered.

No answer. On the TV screen, the embarrassed girl was replaced by a huge airplane zooming closer and closer. . . .

"Grandma!" Dexter screamed.

Grandma bolted upright.

"Wha . . . Huh?" She swung her head frantically side to side, as if she expected to see the room bursting into flames, or a burglar crawling in the window, or a tiger leaping through the doorway. "Dexter, what on earth—?"

Dexter couldn't exactly tell her he'd thought she was dead.

"I, um, finished my homework," he said.

"Well, goodness, that's no reason to yell," Grandma said.

"Were you asleep?" Dexter asked.

"Nonsense. I was just resting my eyes," Grandma said, blinking drowsily. She shoved her glasses back into place, shook her head a little, then patted the couch cushion beside her. "Want to come sit and watch with me?"

Dexter looked doubtfully at the TV. The regular program was back on—an old man warbling some old-fashioned-sounding song.

"I guess not," Grandma said. "Want to go play outside until dinner?"

Dexter thought about Grandma's yard, a little rectangle in the front and an even smaller rectangle in the back.

"Play what?" he asked.

"Um . . . ," she began. Then her expression brightened suddenly. "I know! I still have your uncle Ted's bike in the garage. He used to ride it around the neighborhood all the time after school. Him and Charlie Lincoln and

Franklin Jones and Anthony Teeters—what fun those boys had! I can still see the four of them, riding down the street. . . ."

Grandma had a faraway look on her face now, like she really was back in the past, watching Uncle Ted, a little kid again.

"Land sakes, that must have been thirty years ago," Grandma said, laughing a little. "Here they are, all grown men now, and three of the four of them bald as posts!"

Dexter tried to imagine his uncle Ted riding a bike. Uncle Ted was not just grown-up and bald. He was also so tall that he had to duck his head to walk through doors. On a little-kid bike, his knees would hit his chin and his long arms would dangle over the handlebars, like a clown act in the circus.

Grandma stopped laughing.

"Oops, sorry, I shouldn't have said that, 'bald as posts,'" Grandma said. "I just didn't think."

Dexter remembered who else was bald now: Daddy. The medicine had made him lose his hair. But what had always looked normal and natural and right on Uncle Ted looked strange and scary and sad on Dexter's dad.

"The key to the garage is in the kitchen drawer, right by the sink," Grandma was saying now, quickly. "If you need to put air in any of the tires, the bike pump's beside your grandfather's old tool table."

"Okay," Dexter said. He didn't feel like riding a bike anymore—he hadn't felt like it to begin with. But he couldn't stay here with Grandma right now.

Chapter 6

Dexter got the key from the kitchen drawer and unlocked the garage. He fought his way past Grandma's car, and an old lawn mower, and a bunch of old clay pots. The bike was behind a stack of wood posts. Dexter kicked at the tires—they were pretty flat. But he'd never operated a bike pump before, so he decided he didn't care. By jerking and pulling and yanking, he got the bike out to the drive-way.

Mom and Dad never would have made me do that by myself, he thought. *They would have unlocked the garage for me and held on to the key so I wouldn't lose it. They would have pumped up the tires, to make sure they were safe. They would have made me wear a helmet.*

Angrily, Dexter straddled the bike and kicked one pedal toward the ground. The bike lurched forward. But Dexter had forgotten about the kickstand, so the tires skidded to a halt as soon as the other pedal slammed against it. Dexter would have gone flying over the handlebars if he hadn't been holding on so tightly. As it was, he had to stretch his toe to the ground to keep from falling. The pedal scraped against his leg.

Don't look, Dexter told himself. *Don't look and you can forget you got hurt. See? No pain at all. None.*

Without even glancing down, he used the toe of his shoe to shove the kickstand up and out of the way. Then he began pedaling furiously down the block.

He passed one old house after another. They blurred together, even though Dexter wasn't going very fast.

Mom and Dad never would have let me do

this, he thought. Back home, he wasn't allowed to cross the street by himself. When he rode his bike, he had to stay on the sidewalk in front of his own house. He couldn't go beyond that without a grown-up.

Grandma doesn't care, he told himself.

He came to the corner and let his tire bump down into the street. He rode up the wheelchair ramp on the other side, onto the next sidewalk. He'd done it—he'd crossed the street all by himself and nothing had happened.

So there, he thought.

But it didn't really feel exciting to be out riding a bike all by himself. It felt lonely and scary and sad.

Dexter crossed more streets, and turned a couple corners. He kept telling himself he needed to keep track of where he was going. But he had trouble remembering, especially when he had to work so hard just to push down on the pedals and keep the bike going.

And he was getting a funny idea in his

head that made it hard for him to think about anything else. Maybe, just maybe, it would turn out that Uncle Ted's bike was magic, and Dexter would end up back in Cincinnati if he kept pedaling. And Mom and Dad would be there, and everything would be okay again: Daddy wouldn't be sick and Mommy would have all the time in the world to be a mom. And Dexter never would have had to move in with Grandma or go to a new school or hate everyone or beat up anyone. . . .

"Hey!"

Dexter looked up, half expecting to see his own familiar street in front of him, his own familiar house. But he was in front of a huge park now. The bike hadn't carried Dexter home. Of course it hadn't.

Dexter looked at the little-kid swings and slides in the park. Wait a minute—he remembered this place. Dexter's dad used to bring him here, years ago, those times when they were all visiting Grandma and Dexter would get squirmy sitting on her stiff furniture and trying to be polite.

"We boys just need some run-around time, don't we, Dex?" Dad would say. And then he'd race Dexter across the park, and they'd fall on the ground in a heap, laughing and squealing.

Daddy wouldn't even be able to walk to the park now, Dexter thought, kicking harder than ever at the pedals.

"Hey!" someone said again.

Dexter had already forgotten the first yell, because he'd been too busy thinking about how the bike wasn't magic and how Daddy maybe wouldn't be able to run with him ever again. But this time he looked around, past the swings and slides. Someone was waving at him.

Robin Bryce.

Robin came running toward him. A woman carrying a little brown dog was behind him, trying to keep up.

"You've got blood all over your leg!"

Robin shouted as soon as he was close enough that Dexter could hear him well.

"Do I?" Dexter asked.

He looked down, and there was a stream of blood starting where he'd scraped his leg on the pedal. It ran all the way down to his shoe. The blood was bright red, a shocking color soaking into his white sock. He felt dizzy just looking at it.

"Oh, dear," the woman behind Robin said. "I'm Robin's mom. Can you tell me what happened?"

Dexter shrugged.

"I just hit my leg against the pedal by mistake," he said. "I'm okay."

Robin stared, his eyes almost popping out of his head.

"Wow," he said. "You're really brave."

Dexter felt his face get hot.

"I better go now," he said. "You know— before I bleed any more."

He wasn't sure he could make it back to Grandma's, now that he'd seen what his leg

looked like. Anyhow, the muscles in both his legs ached just from pedaling to the park. And he couldn't quite remember the directions. Had he turned right or left by that house with the yellow awnings?

Still, he was scared that if he stayed here, Robin would say, "See, Mom, this is the boy I was telling you about, the one who beat me up this morning. Aren't you going to call the principal now? Aren't you going to call the police?"

Dexter put his right foot back up on the pedal and started to push off, but Robin's mom dropped the dog and grabbed Dexter's handlebars.

"Oh, no," she said. "You can't ride home with a wound like that. And look—both your tires have gone completely flat."

Dexter looked. The tires didn't look any flatter than they had when he'd started out.

"We live right over there," Robin's mom said, pointing at a small white house at the edge of the park. "Why don't you let me

clean up your wound and give you a Band-
Aid? And then I could drive you home."

"I'm not supposed to go with strangers,"
Dexter said.

Robin looked like he thought Dexter was
being too picky, for someone who was practically bleeding to death. But Robin's mother
nodded and said, "That's a smart boy—you
don't know me at all. Here, let's use my cell
phone and call to have someone pick you up.
What's the number?"

She reached into her pocket and pulled out a
phone. She flipped open the top and held her
finger over the buttons, waiting.

"Um," Dexter said. "It's five-five-five, uh—"
What if he forgot the rest of the number?
What if he said it wrong? "Six-three-eight-one,"
he finished in a rush, praying it was right.

Robin's mom began speaking into the
phone.

"Hello, this is Myrna Bryce. I'm here in the
park with, uh—"

"Dexter," Dexter told her.

"With Dexter," she said. "And he's hurt his leg and it's bleeding quite a bit, and . . ."

Mrs. Bryce seemed to be listening now.

"Oh, no, it's not that bad," she said. "He doesn't need to go to the hospital. It's just, I don't think he could ride his bike with such a bad scrape, and it does need to be cleaned, and I just thought you might want to come and get him. . . ."

She started nodding, like she approved of whatever Dexter's grandmother was saying.

"All right," she said finally. "My son and I will stay here with Dexter until you arrive."

She shut off the phone and put it back into her pocket. Dexter was glad that the dog she'd been carrying began barking just then, because Robin and his mother started looking at the dog instead of him.

"No, Petunia," Robin said. "Be quiet."

The dog kept barking.

"Petunia!" Mrs. Bryce said in a stern voice.

The dog whimpered a little and lay down on its paws.

"He never listens to me," Robin complained. "I bet he'd listen to Dexter."

"Do you have a dog, Dexter?" Mrs. Bryce asked.

Dexter thought about how his parents always used to say that he could get a dog when he was eight. But by the time he turned eight, Daddy was sick. And the one time Dexter had just kind of slightly hinted that maybe, just maybe he should have a dog to make up for Mom and Dad leaving him at Grandma's, Mom had snapped, "Dexter, *really*! Think about it! With everything else that's going on, do you honestly think that anyone has the time or energy for a dog?"

Dexter had wanted to say, "I do." But Mom had already left the room, gone to pack to leave.

"I don't have a dog," he told Mrs. Bryce now in a flat, hopeless voice.

"Well, if it's okay with your parents, you're welcome to come over and play with Petunia sometime. Robin would like that, wouldn't you, Robin?" Mrs. Bryce said.

Dexter knew he should tell her that he lived with his grandmother, not his parents. But he just shrugged and stared at the ground. He felt so tired all of a sudden—so tired he didn't even bother listening to how Robin answered his mother.

Grandma got there quickly, with a hot washcloth in a plastic bag and a whole first-aid kit ready on the front seat of her car. She had Dexter's cut washed, disinfected and bandaged before he knew it.

"You're . . . good at this," Dexter mumbled, leaning his head back against the seat of the car while Grandma knelt at the curb beside him.

Grandma laughed.

"Well, you know, Dexter, I was a mother for many, many years before I became a grandmother."

Grandma went around to the back of the car with Mrs. Bryce. They had the trunk open and were turning Uncle Ted's bike this way and that, trying to figure out the best way to put it in. Dexter could hear them talking, but he couldn't quite hear what they were saying. Robin stayed right by Dexter's side.

"I would have fainted, bleeding like that," he said. "Didn't it hurt? Didn't you want to cry?"

Dexter shrugged.

"I didn't notice," he said.

He could have said, "My dad's really, really sick, and my mom left me with my grandma, and I can't have a dog, and I had to go to a horrible new school today, and I hated everyone there, and I'm just lucky the police didn't arrest me for fighting, and maybe they still will. . . . And you think I should cry over a stupid little scrape?"

Except, saying that probably would make him cry.

"I wish I was like you," Robin said, biting his lip.

Grandma and Mrs. Bryce came back around to the front of the car.

"It'd take someone with an engineering degree to fit that bike in the trunk," Grandma said. "Mrs. Bryce says they can keep the bike in their garage until your leg's healed enough that you can ride it home. Myrna, thanks so much, I really appreciate all you've done. If you hadn't been here to help—"

"Oh, Dexter would have managed," Mrs. Bryce said, waving away the thanks. "He seems like a very self-sufficient little boy."

Grandma slipped into the driver's seat, and pulled the car away from the curb. Dexter still had his window rolled down— that was the only reason he heard what Robin was saying to Mrs. Bryce.

"See, Mom, that's the boy I was telling you about. . . ."

The wind caught the rest of Robin's words, so Dexter couldn't hear anything else. But he didn't need to. He slumped against the seat.

Now Mrs. Bryce knows I beat up Robin, he thought. *I won't ever be able to get that bike*

back. I won't ever be able to play with Robin's dog. I won't ever be able to come to the park again, because they might see me. Oh, why did Robin have to be the kid I beat up?

Chapter 7

I'm the new kid. This morning I beat up
Robin Bryce. In the bathroom. The one
between the office and your classroom.
With the blue tile on the wall. I was mad.

The teacher, Ms. Abbott, sat reading
Dexter's story. She wasn't twinkling, the
way she had during math, and spelling, and
health, and everything else they'd talked
about the entire day. Her eyebrows squinted
together.

"This is better," she said finally. "You're
definitely going in the right direction."

"Then I'm done?" Dexter asked.

That made Ms. Abbott laugh and almost—but just almost—sparkle.

"Oh, no," she said. "Remember, we're acting like professional writers, and professional writers do lots and lots and lots of drafts. And you know what? You should save every draft, so you can see the progress you're making." She pointed at the *X* Dexter had drawn through his original story. "You shouldn't be ashamed of old drafts, just because they're not perfect. Writing is a *process.*"

She studied Dexter's words again.

"What do you think of this version of your story?" she asked.

"I don't know," Dexter said. "It's okay, I guess."

"Let's pretend you weren't the one who wrote it," Ms. Abbott said. "Pretend you just found this story somewhere and you read it. What would you think the writer thought was the most important part of the whole story?"

Dexter shrugged. He looked longingly at

his own desk, where he'd been working on a punctuation work sheet before Ms. Abbott called him up to talk about his story. He wasn't a big fan of punctuation work sheets, but they were much, much better than this.

"What does the writer of this story spend the most time describing?" Ms. Abbott asked, still acting like Dexter wasn't the writer.

Dexter frowned down at his story. He wished it did belong to someone else.

"The bathroom?" he asked.

"Bingo!" Ms. Abbott said. "Good job! You win the prize! Now for the really hard question, I need Dexter the author back. Dexter, for the all-expense-paid trip to Hawaii and the side-by-side washer-dryer, tell me the most important thing about this fight. Was it the fact that it took place in the bathroom?"

"No," Dexter muttered.

Dexter hoped that Ms. Abbott would get even sillier, pretending to be a game-show host awarding the grand prize. He hoped that she would forget that they were talking about his story. But she just nodded and said, "Then what was it?"

Dexter looked down at his lap. He had his hands clenched together—his left hand was holding down the hand that had hit Robin.

"Dexter?" Ms. Abbott said softly. "This is a question only you know the answer to. I can only guess about why this fight was important. Does it have something to do with the reason you were mad? Was it what Robin said or did before you beat him up? Was it how you felt after you hit him? I think that's the question you need to think about for your next revision. It's a big question, so I'll only give you one."

She wrote one sentence in her perfect cursive at the bottom of the page. Then she handed the paper back to Dexter.

"And if I forget, will you remind me that we need to talk about sentence fragments as a whole class?" she said, smiling again.

Dexter went back to his desk. He looked at his story again. He knew what sentence fragments were. He'd learned about them at his old school. They were little parts of a sentence that got cut off from the rest of the sentence, that weren't supposed to stand alone. They were things like, "In the bathroom." And "The one between the office and your classroom." Practically his whole story was sentence fragments, all those little phrases that couldn't survive on their own.

Dexter's eyes blurred. There was something really, really wrong with him. Now he was feeling sorry for sentence fragments.

Chapter 8

Dexter hid out around the corner of the school during recess. There, he could kick pebbles without the playground monitor watching him. But he peeked out a couple times, just to make sure no one was coming for him.

It was a good thing he did that. The third or fourth time he looked out, he saw Ms. Abbott walk out of the school building and make a beeline for the playground monitor. They talked together for a few minutes, then the playground monitor pointed far, far past the tetherball courts and the kickball field, almost to the edge of the school yard. She was pointing to a boy huddled in the grass back by a bunch of bushes.

She was pointing at Robin Bryce.

Ms. Abbott nodded and began hurrying toward Robin.

Dexter gasped. His heart began pounding, like it wanted to burst completely out of his chest and explode right there all over the pebbles. He took off running—blindly at first, but then with a purpose. He darted into the bushes that surrounded the school grounds.

Good place to hide . . . have to get there first . . . can't let them see me . . .

He had to slow down when he turned the corner. Staying in the bushes, he crept closer and closer to where Robin was sitting. He peeked out and was sure he was too late.

Ms. Abbott was already there.

She was crouched down beside Robin.

"No," Robin was saying. "Me and Dexter are friends. Sort of. We were at the park together last night."

"Then he didn't hurt you yesterday morning? In the bathroom, before school?" Ms. Abbott asked.

See, Ms. Abbott really does think it matters where the fight happened, Dexter thought. *And she knows now that I was lying . . .*

He couldn't hear Robin's answer. Desperate, Dexter shoved leaves out of the way, trying to see Robin's face.

Robin was turned the other way. But Dexter could tell from behind: Robin was shaking his head.

He was shaking his head no.

"Okay, then," Ms. Abbott said, standing up. "Sorry to bother you. I'm very glad to hear that there wasn't a fight. I just had to make sure."

"You don't know where Dexter is now, do you?" Robin asked, looking up at her. "I was kind of hoping . . ."

Ms. Abbott gazed across the playground, squinting into the sun. She lifted her hand to shield her eyes.

"Sorry," she said. "I don't know where he is. He's got to be around here somewhere."

And then Dexter knew he was about to snort with laughter and relief. He pulled back deeper into the bushes, and stuffed his hand over his mouth to keep from making any noise.

Long after Robin and Ms. Abbott moved away, Dexter stayed in the bushes, shaking. He couldn't have said anymore what he was holding in, with his hand over his mouth.

Robin lied for me, Dexter thought. *He told his mother what I did, but he lied to Ms. Abbott. Why?*

And why would he say we were friends?

Chapter 9

I'm the new kid. On my first day here at King Elementary School I beat up Robin Bryce. We were in the bathroom, but that doesn't matter. I was mad, but that doesn't matter either. The whole fight doesn't matter. It was no big deal.

"Hmm . . . ," Ms. Abbott said.

Dexter waited, trying not to squirm in the chair beside Ms. Abbott's desk. It had been three days since the last time he'd workshopped with Ms. Abbott. She'd said that morning that she was getting a little behind.

"But that's okay—don't worry," she'd

told the class with a little laugh. "Lots of professional writers will take time off between drafts, to think more deeply about their work."

Dexter felt kind of proud of this version of his story. It didn't contain a single sentence fragment. He thought Ms. Abbott would be impressed that he'd put in "King Elementary School"—giving an exact name. And this draft told Ms. Abbott, and anyone else who might read it, that the fight didn't matter. It wasn't worth worrying about.

This was a safe story now.

Dexter was feeling safer all around. He'd gotten really good at hiding out at recess. Thanks to the bushes, Robin would never be able to find him. When Mrs. Bryce called to see when Dexter was going to come over to get his bike, Dexter told Grandma to say his leg still hurt too much. He planned to let his leg keep hurting for a very, very long time. As far as he was concerned, the Bryces could just keep Uncle Ted's bike.

Because of his hurt leg, Dexter was spending a lot of time in the house, watching TV with Grandma. Even when Mom or Dad called, Dexter just said, "Uh-huh," and "Unh-unhh," and "Sure. Fine." He didn't ask any questions. He kept his eyes on the commercials for toilet paper and Pepto-Bismol and aspirin the whole time he was on the phone.

"Hmm . . . ," Ms. Abbott said again. "I think it's time to try something different."

"What do you mean?" Dexter asked.

"Sometimes professional writers experiment a little with their work," Ms. Abbott said. "Sometimes they'll write a scene from a different perspective, to see if things sound different. To help them understand all their characters' viewpoints. Sometimes they'll even pretend to be, like, a fly on the wall, watching the action."

"There weren't any flies in the bathroom," Dexter said. He didn't know why, but he could feel panic rising in his stomach.

Ms. Abbott gave him a strange look.

"You could always pretend," she said. "This is an imaginary fight you're writing about anyhow, right?"

"Uh, right," Dexter said. This wasn't helping his panic.

"Maybe you mean that flies just wouldn't fit with the spirit of the story," Ms. Abbott said. "They'd change the mood too much."

"Yeah," Dexter said. "That."

Ms. Abbott looked down at his story.

"I agree with you," she said. "That wasn't what I had in mind, anyhow. I was thinking that you should try writing the whole story from Robin's point of view. Pretend you're him. Tell about the whole incident as *he* experienced it."

That did it. Now Dexter's panic was on the verge of boiling over. Any minute now he might start throwing up, or screaming, or crying, or running out of the room.

"I'm not Robin," Dexter said. "Really, I don't even know him."

Ms. Abbott tapped her finger against Dexter's forehead.

"That's what your imagination's for," she said.

She sat back, her eyes boring into Dexter's. Dexter had to work very hard to hold his panic down, to keep from letting her see how upset he was.

"Or," she said slowly, "you could ask him to help."

Chapter 10

Dexter wasn't asking anyone for help. He sat hunched over his paper at Grandma's kitchen table.

If I was Robin Bryce...

No. Erase, try again.

You said I had to pretend to be Robin Bryce, so...

Erase again.

Finally, after his eraser made holes in the paper and he had to skip down to the next line, he wrote simply:

I am being Robin Bryce.

He sat back, trying to think what that would be like. He squinted down at his hand holding the pencil. He wanted to trick his eyes into seeing his hands and arms as bigger and flabbier and paler, covered with Robin's pasty white skin.

I am big but I am not strong. I have comb tracks in my hair when I get to school in the morning.

That was describing Robin, not telling about the fight. But Dexter didn't erase any of it. He pressed his pencil down harder and added:

Last Monday I was in the bathroom before school started. This skinny little kid came in and beat me up. I found out later his name was Dexter.

Dexter sat back in his chair, thinking. Something was missing. He heard the phone ring in the living room. Quickly, before he had time to get distracted, he wrote:

Robin was crying before Dexter hit him.

"Dexter!" Grandma yelled from the living room. "Telephone!"

Dexter flipped his paper over upside down, as if he thought whoever was on the phone might be able to see it.

"I can't talk right now," he hollered back to Grandma. "I'm doing homework!"

Grandma appeared in the doorway.

"It's your dad," she said.

Usually Dad didn't call. Usually it was just his mom, calling from the hospital hallway or waiting room. Usually Dad was in too much pain to talk.

Dexter took the phone.

"Hello?" he whispered, like he thought talking loud might hurt Dad's ears.

"Hey, Dex," Dad said weakly. "You know, I'm starting the experimental treatment tomorrow. And it's going to make me really, really sick for a while."

Dexter didn't know how Dad could get any sicker.

"I thought you weren't going to have to do that," Dexter protested. "I thought they were going to give you the marshmallow transplant."

"Bone marrow," Dad said. "Remember? Bone marrow's the stuff that makes your blood."

Dexter knew that. If he let himself think about it, he knew a lot of facts about blood and how his dad's didn't work right. But he wanted his dad to laugh the way he'd laughed last summer, when Mom and Dad were talking about bone marrow transplant this and bone marrow transplant that, and Dexter had accidentally flubbed the name. It became a family joke—Dexter had even drawn a picture of Dad eating globs of

marshmallow fluff, and telling it, "Don't go to my stomach! Go to my bones!"

Then they'd found out that nobody in the family had the right kind of bone marrow to give to Dad. Nobody they knew matched.

"I thought they were looking all over the world for someone to help you," Dexter said.

"They are," Dad said. "But I can't wait forever. I've got to try this other treatment because . . . because . . . right now it's my only chance."

Dexter swallowed hard. There wasn't anything he could say to that.

"And, Dexter?" Dad said. "Before I do this, I just wanted to tell you . . . I love you very, very much. You know that, don't you?"

"Yes," Dexter whispered.

"I am so proud of you. I feel so lucky to have such a wonderful son."

Dexter bent his head down, because he

didn't want Grandma to see how he'd lost control of his face all of a sudden. He could feel it twisting and bunching up, his mouth opening like it had decided on its own that he needed to let out a huge wail. But bending his head meant that Dexter was looking right at his homework paper now. Even though it was upside down, the paper was thin enough that he could still see through the other side. He could still read "Dexter hit Robin" upside down and backward.

Daddy wouldn't be proud of me if he knew what I did, Dexter thought. *He wouldn't think I was a wonderful son then.*

Dexter slid his hand over the top of his homework paper. But that didn't seem like enough, so he crossed his arms over the paper and leaned forward so he was practically lying on it, his ear pressed against the phone.

"No matter what happens . . . ," Dad was saying.

Dexter couldn't listen. He was concentrating too hard on covering over those awful words. And he was concentrating too hard on holding himself together—not wailing, not screaming, not throwing the phone down, not ripping the paper up. Not crying.

"Good-bye for now," Daddy said. Dexter nodded, even though he knew Daddy couldn't see him.

The phone clicked, then the dial tone came on, too loud and buzzing. Somehow Dexter couldn't bring himself to let go of the phone.

Grandma stepped up beside him and eased the phone away from his ear. She slipped the homework paper out from under his arms and into his backpack. And then she did a funny thing. She sat down in a chair and lifted Dexter into her lap. She put her arms around him and held him tight, like he was a really little kid. A baby, even.

Dexter didn't mind at all.

Chapter 11

"Dexter, I am so excited to see what you wrote," Ms. Abbott said, beaming at him.

Dexter blinked up at her.

"Huh?" he asked.

He was in a daze today. He kept wondering what time Daddy was starting the experimental treatment. Why hadn't Dexter asked? Maybe right this very minute Daddy was being wheeled into an operating room, or hooked up to some nasty medicine that would make him throw up and sweat and shiver even worse than ever. Dexter had seen Daddy get sick from medicine so many times before. Maybe this time he would even . . .

"Your *story*," Ms. Abbott said, grinning and flipping a strand of her long, honey-colored hair over her shoulder. "Remember?"

Today, being in the same room with Ms. Abbott felt like staring into the sun. She glowed so brightly it hurt to look. Today Dexter belonged in a dark room, with all the shades drawn. Last night at bedtime Grandma had turned out the lights and sat on the edge of Dexter's bed. She'd clutched his hand and prayed, over and over again: "Lord, please be with your son Thomas, Dexter's daddy. Please wrap this whole family in your love. Please guide the doctor's hands. Please, God, Dexter and his momma need Thomas here. . . ."

And lying in the dark, listening to Grandma pray, Dexter had felt that maybe there was still some hope. He'd fallen asleep listening to Grandma talking to God.

But then this morning Grandma had to go to work and Dexter had to go to school, like usual. Like nothing important was happening today. And in the sunlight, Dexter couldn't hold the sound of Grandma's prayers in his head anymore.

"Dexter," Ms. Abbott said. "You did write another version of your story, didn't you? Telling Robin's side of things?"

A stern tone had crept into her voice. She had her hands on her hips.

"Yeah," Dexter said dully. He remembered Grandma putting the paper in his backpack. "I'll get it."

He went to the cubbyhole where he'd stored his backpack. Unzip the backpack, pull out the paper, walk back to Ms. Abbott . . . everything seemed to take an extra effort.

Ms. Abbott was watching him, her eyebrows squinted together.

"Thank you," she said, sounding puzzled now. She took the paper and let him sit down in the chair by her desk.

Dexter watched Ms. Abbott read. What had he written? Oh, yeah, about how Robin saw the fight.

Suddenly Ms. Abbott's eyes got really big and her eyebrows arched up toward her hair.

"He was already crying?" she asked. "Before you hit him?"

"Yeah," Dexter said.

"You hit Robin Bryce when he was crying?"

Dexter shrugged. Ms. Abbott put down the paper and stared at him, her mouth hanging open, like she didn't know what to say. That look broke through Dexter's daze.

Oh, no, Dexter thought. *Grandma was praying so hard for Daddy, telling God I need my daddy alive. Why would God want to do something nice for me? I'm a terrible person. I beat up Robin. I beat him up when he was already crying.*

Dexter thought his face was going to burn up with shame.

"In the story," he told Ms. Abbott quickly. "It's just a story, that he was crying and I beat him up."

Ms. Abbott swallowed hard. She winced a

little. But when she spoke again, her voice was gentle.

"Why was Robin crying?" she asked.

Dexter shrugged again.

"You don't know?" Ms. Abbott said.

Dexter shook his head no.

"Then find out," Ms. Abbott said. "That's your assignment for tomorrow, *find out*."

Chapter 12

Dexter knew he was going to have to ask
Robin. At recess, after all the other kids had
raced outside, Dexter trudged down the hall
and through the doors. He came to a stop in
the too-bright sunshine.

Robin was not sitting in his usual spot
over by the bushes.

Dexter circled the playground. He looked
in the bushes. He stared at every kid on
every swing and slide.

He heard something hitting the building
near his old hiding place around the corner.
He tiptoed through the pebbles and peeked
around the building.

Now it was Robin kicking stones at the school.

"You'll get in trouble for that," Dexter said.

Robin paused mid-kick. He looked at Dexter, then went ahead and sent another burst of pebbles sailing toward the wall.

"This is what *you* do," he said.

"I used to," Dexter agreed. "But I wasn't so loud."

Robin stopped kicking stones.

"Nobody will play with me," he said.

"So?" Dexter said.

"So who cares if I kick stones at the school or not?"

Dexter didn't. He shrugged, like it didn't matter at all.

Then he remembered what he needed to ask Robin. He gulped.

"You were crying," he began.

"I was not!" Robin snapped. He stuck his face right up close to Dexter's. "Do my eyes look red? Do you see any tears?"

"I mean, last week," Dexter said, backing away from Robin. "In the bathroom."

"Oh," Robin said, his shoulders sagging.

"I didn't know why you were crying," Dexter said.

"What's it to you?" Robin snarled.

It was too complicated to explain about the story, and Ms. Abbott's questions, and how professional writers work. And maybe that wasn't even Dexter's reason. He had too much mixed up in his mind. He could see his fist hitting Robin's jaw, again and again and again, like a scene from a DVD being played over and over. He could see the comb tracks Robin had had in his hair that day. He could see the tears streaming down Robin's face. He could see the crowd of kids laughing at him when he fell. He could see his father's body, not moving, just a lump under the sheet of a hospital bed. He could see Grandma's arms wrapped around him while she prayed. He could see Ms. Abbott's horrified face when she asked,

"You hit Robin Bryce when he was crying?"

"I just want to know," Dexter said.

Robin slumped against the building. He slid down, like his legs couldn't hold him up anymore. He ended up sitting in the stones.

Dexter sat down beside him.

"Why were you crying?" he said.

Robin let his chin fall against his knees.

"I hate school," he said.

"Oh, me too," Dexter said quickly.

"You do?" Robin asked, almost sounding happy about it.

"Yeah," Dexter said. "I hate the principal, and the secretary, and the janitor, and my teacher, and all the other kids."

"Maybe I don't hate that many people," Robin said. He picked up a pebble and sent it skipping through the other stones. "It's just, I thought it would be fun, you know? I never went to school before this year."

"You're a kindergartener?" Dexter gasped. It was awful that Robin could be so much bigger and taller than Dexter, and just be in kindergarten.

It was awful that Dexter could have beaten up a poor little kindergartener who was already crying before Dexter hit him.

"No," Robin said, sounding annoyed. "I'm in fourth grade. But Mom always home-schooled me before."

Dexter's mom didn't even have time to live in the same house with him. But Robin's mom cared enough to comb his hair perfectly every morning, and let him have a dog, *and* be his teacher for kindergarten through third grade.

"Bet your mom got tired of that," Dexter said in a mean voice. "Bet she was really glad to send you out the door to school."

"No," Robin said. "She wanted to keep homeschooling me. But I begged and begged to go to school. Every time we drove past the school, every time I saw kids on the school bus—everyone always looked so happy. I thought I'd have so many friends. . . ."

"So why don't you?" Dexter asked.

Robin stared down at the stones. For a minute Dexter didn't think he was going to answer. Then he looked up.

"How do you make friends?" he asked earnestly. "How does it work?"

Dexter had never thought about it. Back home, he'd just *had* friends, he hadn't had to work at it. And here—he hadn't wanted friends. The other kids had stopped asking him to play kickball after that first day.

"Well, you just, uh . . ." Dexter fumbled for a way to explain it to Robin. "Let's say you want to play basketball. So you just go up to a kid and say, 'Wanna shoot hoops?' And if he says yes, then you play. And if he says no, then you ask someone else."

"But everybody already hates me," Robin said. "Right away, the first day of school, they started making fun of my name. And after that, well—" He glanced sideways at Dexter, then looked away fast. "Some kids saw me crying, and they called

me a crybaby. And that made me cry more."

"So you were crying because some kids called you a crybaby?" Dexter asked.

"No!—er, kind of, I mean—I just wanted to go home. I missed my mom. I didn't want to go to school anymore! I wanted to be home-schooled again. But I couldn't tell my mom that, not after I begged so hard. . . ."

Dexter didn't know how Robin could miss his mom when he got to see her every morn-ing and every afternoon after school. She probably tucked him into bed every night. She probably fixed his breakfast, and packed his lunches, and oohed and aahed over his home-work papers every day.

Dexter hadn't seen either of his parents in almost two weeks. His mom had left him behind. His dad was so sick that regular med-icine didn't work on him, and the doctors had to try an experiment. All Dexter had right now was Grandma. And, sure, she was good at praying and putting on Band-Aids. But she wore those old-lady clothes and she was always tired after work. And she still didn't know that Dexter hated graham crackers, and canned pears, and old men singing on TV.

Dexter started to stand up, because he couldn't take it anymore, poor little Robin whining about being away from his stupid mom for a couple of hours a day. But suddenly Robin looked over at Dexter and asked, "So maybe I was crying. But why were you so mad?"

"Huh?" Dexter said, caught half up and half down.

"That day in the bathroom. You were mad before you saw me. I could tell, because of the way you walked in—"

He hopped up and did an imitation, scowling and hunching up his shoulders and stomping his feet.

Dexter couldn't help himself. He laughed.

"I wasn't that bad!" he complained.

"Yes, you were!"

"Well, a bunch of kids laughed at me because I fell down," Dexter said. "The janitor made the floor too slippery. That's why I said I hated him.

And the principal was mean to me, and it was my first day of school and the secretary started to show me where to go but then she just left me standing there, in the middle of the hall. And I didn't know what I was supposed to do."

Dexter hadn't planned to tell Robin any of that, but the words just came tumbling out. He had to shut his mouth tight to keep from telling the rest, about Dad and Mom and Grandma and the dog that Dexter wasn't allowed to have. . . .

"Wow," Robin said. "That's bad. At least it's just the kids who have been mean to me. All the grown-ups have been nice."

"Well," Dexter said. "You're a lot luckier than me."

"I guess so," Robin said.

He kept standing there, like he was waiting for something.

"Um, Dexter?" he started to say. "Do you—"

But Ms. Abbott came around the corner just then.

"Dexter! I've been looking all over the place for you. There's a phone call for you. They transferred it to my room—"

Dexter took off running.

Chapter 13

Ms. Abbott had left the phone just dangling from the wall. It took Dexter two tries to scoop it up.

"Hello?" he whispered into the receiver.

"Oh, Dexter," Mom said on the other end of the line. "I've got the best news! The bone marrow transplant—they found a donor!"

"They did?" Dexter was so surprised, he almost dropped the phone. "But Dad said they couldn't! He said—"

"I know, I know!" Mom said, and she was almost laughing now. Dexter couldn't remember the last time he'd heard her laugh. "But, it's like, the doctors wanted to double-check and triple-check the registry before they started him on the experimental treatment, and something new turned up, a donor in Kansas, someone who must have just signed up—"

"Daddy has to go to Kansas?" Dexter asked. He tried to remember exactly where Kansas was.

"No, no, they'll ship the marrow to the hospital here—oh, Dexter, isn't this wonderful?"

Dexter was trying to take it all in. He still felt dazed, like his feelings hadn't caught up with the news.

"Then you'll come home?" he said. "And we'll be . . . just like before?"

He meant, before Daddy got sick. He could picture him and Mom and Dad living in their house in Cincinnati again, Dexter going to his old school, playing with his old friends at recess, Daddy sometimes even coming out and playing football with them in the yard . . . It would be like nothing bad had ever happened.

"Well, it's going to be a while still, but,

yes, that's what we're working toward," Mom said. "This could completely cure Daddy, so he'll never be sick again. Can you imagine? No more living out of hospital rooms, no more chemo making him throw up, no more being apart from you. . . ."

Dexter tightened his grip on the phone.

"You don't like being away?"

"Dexter! Haven't you been listening every night when we tell you how much we miss you?"

Actually, Dexter hadn't. Or, if he'd been listening, it hadn't really sunk in.

"I thought maybe you liked Seattle," he said.

"Oh, please!" Mom said. "Did you think I've been sightseeing? Going up in the Space Needle? Hiking at Mount Rainier? I've barely left the hospital. And that's okay—I want to be here with Dad. He . . . needs me. But I hate being away from you, and I can't wait until Daddy's better and we can all go home. That's why this is the most incredible news—aren't you excited?"

"Yeah," Dexter said, except "excited" wasn't quite the right word. It was more like he had hope bubbling up inside him now, hope for things he hadn't even let himself think about before.

"When Daddy gets better," he began slowly. "When you come home—when we're all back at our house together . . . then can I get a dog?"

The words just slipped out. Dexter bit his tongue, afraid that Mom would think he was being selfish, that he didn't really care about Daddy. But the dog was his test. If they let him get a dog, that would mean that everything was really okay.

Mom didn't get upset. She started laughing again, sending bursts of giggles through the phone.

"Oh, Dexter," she sputtered, gasping for air. "Oh, Dexter—yes!"

Chapter 14

Grandma wanted to celebrate.

"Think we should throw a party?" she asked when Dexter got home from school. "Want to invite some friends? How about that boy you met in the park?"

"Nn-oo," Dexter said slowly.

"Okay, just us," Grandma said. "I understand. Want to order pizza? Ribs? As far as I'm concerned, tonight you can have all the ice cream you want. . . ."

The phone rang just then.

"Yes, yes," Grandma said into the receiver. "You heard right. We're so happy . . ."

Dexter walked over to the kitchen window

while she was talking. The window looked out on Grandma's garage, where she'd kept Uncle Ted's bike before she let Dexter ride it. Maybe she'd never get it back now, because Dexter was too ashamed to go over to the Bryces' to get it.

Grandma hung up from her phone call.

"That was Marilyn Dowd, who lived next door when your mom was a little girl," she said. "And that reminds me"—she began dialing—"I should let Peggy Fristian know, too. . . ."

This time while Grandma was on the phone, Dexter pulled his story out of his backpack. Ms. Abbott had told him that, because of the big news, she'd give him an extension on his story. He wouldn't have to turn it in until next week.

"You probably don't feel like concentrating on schoolwork right now," she'd said.

Ms. Abbott hadn't known until today that Dexter's dad needed a bone marrow transplant. She didn't know that Dexter hadn't felt like concentrating on schoolwork since Dad got sick.

On the phone, Grandma was telling Peggy Fristian—whoever that was—"I just had to share the good news! Of course we still have to pray for Thomas's complete recovery, but this is such a miracle. . . ."

Dexter reread his story, all the way up to the last line: Robin was crying before Dexter hit him.

The thing was, Dexter did kind of want Robin to come over and celebrate. He wanted Robin to know that Dexter's dad was going to be okay. He wanted Robin to know that Dexter's mom hadn't just left him behind for no good reason. He wanted Robin to know that Dexter was going to get a dog. He even wanted to tell Robin the jokes about transplanting marshmallow fluff.

But Dexter had *hit* Robin. Dexter had beaten Robin up. And Robin had told his mom about it, and there was no way Robin's mom would want Robin hanging around with Dexter now.

Dexter remembered how he thought that when Dad and Mom came home, it would be like nothing bad had ever happened. Dexter didn't really understand how a bone marrow transplant worked—he thought it was kind of like a do-over in basketball, where Daddy's body would get a whole new chance to make good blood, instead of bad.

There wasn't any kind of a transplant that could undo Dexter beating up Robin.

How could Mom and Dad have such good news, when everything was still so messed up for Dexter?

Chapter 15

"Psst."

It was time for recess, the next day. Dexter was just walking out of the school—last, as usual. The "Psst," came from behind the door, then there was a whisper, "Hey, Dexter. Over here."

Dexter let the door swing shut. Robin was crammed in behind the door, like some sort of secret agent.

"I've got someone for you to talk to," Robin whispered. "Follow me."

Robin yanked the door open again and slipped inside.

"I don't think we're supposed to—," Dexter started to say.

Robin poked his head out the door.

"What? I can't hear you through the glass. Come on. Hurry up!"

Dexter sighed and followed Robin. Who had ever heard of anyone sneaking back *into* a school building during recess?

Robin led Dexter away from the fourth-grade hallway, into a part of the building that Dexter had never seen before. Judging from the crooked finger paintings hanging on the wall, it was probably the kindergarten wing.

"There he is," Robin said softly.

A man with a broom was sweeping dirt into a dustpan.

"Mr. Chandler, this is the kid I was telling you about," Robin said. "Mr. Chandler, this is Dexter. Dexter, this is Mr. Chandler."

Mr. Chandler was young and had a pony-tail that hung halfway down his back. He had a bandana wrapped around his head, like a pirate.

"Nice to meet you, Dexter," Mr. Chandler said, holding out his hand. "From what Robin tells me, I think I owe you an apology. Something about polishing the floors too well?"

"Uh . . . ," Dexter said. He didn't know what else to do, except shake Mr. Chandler's hand.

"Mr. Chandler's the janitor," Robin said. "He's really a nice guy."

"Yeah, I felt terrible when Robin told me about you falling down your very first day here," Mr. Chandler said. "Think I should change the brand of floor wax we use?"

Dexter shrugged. Robin started nodding like crazy.

"I've got an idea," Robin said. "Maybe Dexter and me could help you try out the different kinds, see what works best without getting too slippery. Could we?"

"Sure," Mr. Chandler said. "I always like having helpers."

"See?" Robin told Dexter. "Didn't I tell you he was nice?"

Dexter flushed red. What if Robin had

told Mr. Chandler that Dexter hated him?

"It wasn't just falling down that made me mad," he mumbled. "The secretary was mean to me, too."

"Oh, right, she went off and left you in the middle of the hall," Robin said. "And you didn't know where you were or what you were supposed to do."

"Betty Sue did that?" Mr. Chandler said. He looked shocked. "Betty Sue's the nicest person I've ever met. She wouldn't leave a new kid alone when . . . Wait a minute— when was your first day?"

"Monday. A week ago," Dexter said.

"Ooh," Mr. Chandler said. "I bet I know what happened, then."

"What?" Robin asked.

"Well, one day last week—it had to have been Monday—Betty Sue caught that stomach bug that's been going around," Mr. Chandler said. "She kept having to run to the bathroom to throw up. She said she wanted to finish up her work before she went home to rest and get better. And—I remember now—she said she threw up for the first time right before the first bell rang. That must have been when she was taking you to your class. But Betty Sue would have apologized. She wouldn't have been mean about it."

Dexter narrowed his eyes, staring at some kindergartener's mess of red and blue paint. Now that he thought about it, he remembered that the secretary had looked pale and clammy. And she'd had beads of sweat on her upper lip, right before she'd run away, leaving him behind. And she'd said something, but Dexter hadn't really heard her. It'd been right then that he'd stepped forward and his feet had flown out from under him, and he'd crashed to the ground and all those kids had laughed at him. And then he'd run into the bathroom.

And when he came out of the bathroom, and saw the secretary again, maybe she had said something. Maybe she'd made all kinds of apologies. Dexter hadn't been able to listen to anything then, because his ears were buzzing and his eyes were blurry.

And his hand hurt, from hitting Robin.

"Maybe you should talk to Betty Sue," Mr. Chandler was saying now. "She'd feel really bad if she knew you were still upset. She'd probably bake you some chocolate chip cookies to make it up to you." He grinned. "If she does, will you share some with me?"

It was hard to hate Mr. Chandler when he was grinning like that. And it was hard to hate anyone named Betty Sue.

"That's okay," Dexter mumbled, staring at his shoes. "I'm not mad anymore."

"That's great," Mr. Chandler said, stepping forward to pick up his dustpan. "Now, if you don't mind, I really need to finish this hallway before the afternoon kindergarteners—"

Mid-stride, one of his feet shot out from under him. His arms flailed backward, like he was trying to grab for the broom to hold himself up. But the broom flipped over and

landed on the handle of the dustpan. It flipped over, too, sending an arc of dust flying up into the air. The dust landed right on top of Mr. Chandler. Flakes of dirt hung in his eyelashes.

Dexter didn't mean to laugh, but it was impossible not to. The giggles came bursting out of him. Robin was laughing, too.

"Oh, sorry, Mr. Chandler," Robin managed to say, between giggles. "We shouldn't—are you all right?"

Mr. Chandler stood up and brushed himself off. He took off his bandana and shook the dust from it down into the dustpan.

"That's okay. You can't be a janitor and be afraid of a little dirt. And—I guess I deserved that for polishing the floor so much that even *I* slip on it. We're testing new floor cleaners, tomorrow, you hear? And—" He rubbed his elbow, the part that had hit the floor the hardest. "I definitely need your help!"

Chapter 16

Dexter sat at Grandma's kitchen table. With the graham cracker box and two cans of pears, he built a little fortress around his homework paper. He glanced once toward the living room, where Grandma had the TV turned up loud. If he leaned forward a little, he could see her on the couch, slumped over. This time, he wasn't scared that she was dead. In fact, he was glad she was sleeping. That meant she wouldn't see what he was working on.

The reason Robin was crying was because he was homesick. And kids

teased him about his name and called
him a crybaby. And he'd never gone to
school before, just had his mom teach
him. And he didn't know how to make
friends. And . . .

What was he supposed to write next?
"And so I hit him"?

Dexter crumpled the paper and hid it
behind the graham cracker box. He got out
another sheet of paper. He smoothed it
down flat and started over.

Robin had lots of reasons for crying. None
of them had anything to do with me. It wasn't
my fault he was crying.
    I had lots of reasons for being mad, too.
The secretary . . .

Dexter stopped again. He'd sound really
stupid if he said he was mad at the secretary
for getting sick. That'd be as bad as saying he
was mad at Dad for getting sick.

Wait a minute. *Had* he been mad at Dad for getting sick?

Dexter crumpled up that piece of paper, too. He tried again.

A bunch of kids laughed at me . . .

Except, Dexter had laughed, too, when Mr. Chandler slipped and fell. He'd looked so funny, spinning his arms in the air, pumping his legs like someone in a cartoon. *Nobody* could have watched that without laughing.

Maybe Dexter had looked even funnier.

Another balled-up piece of paper joined the others behind the graham cracker box.

Dexter pulled out one more sheet of paper and stared at it. It was blank and white and empty. It stayed empty. The longer it stayed empty, the angrier Dexter got. Finally he picked up his pencil and scrawled:

This is a STUPID asinement. Nobody
should have to do this. It's dumb. Really,
really, really dumb!!!!!

He'd never in a million years hand that in.
But it made him feel better to write it down.

Chapter 17

"I am *not* going to go talk to the principal!" Dexter snapped.

Robin was bugging him again at recess. He'd found Dexter's hiding place in the bushes, and crawled in behind him.

"But, see," Robin said, pushing leaves out of his face, "my mom says she has a lot of respect for Mr. Wiseman. And she says she can't imagine him being mean to a new student on purpose, for no reason. So it must just be uh, a misunderstanding, and he'll apologize, just like Mr. Chandler did. And you'll feel better—"

"Wait a minute," Dexter said, jerking

upright so fast that he bumped his head on a branch. "You told your mom that the principal was mean to me?"

"Ye-essss," Robin said slowly.

"Why'd you go and do a stupid thing like that?"

Robin backed up a little.

"Because . . . I thought she could help." he said. "And . . . I didn't know what else to do. And . . . my mom always helps me."

Dexter glared at him.

"You're such a *baby*," he said. "Don't you know, by the time you're in fourth grade, you shouldn't have to go running to Mommy for every little thing?"

Robin glared back. Or tried to. His eyes were starting to look a little too watery to hold a good glare.

"This isn't a little thing," he said in a choked voice. "If a principal's mean to kids—that's wrong! My mom says sometimes principals even get fired for things like that. And if he was really, really nasty, maybe you should even file a complaint with the school board, so he can be kicked out, so he's not mean to anyone else. It's like . . . like why we put criminals in jail, so they can't hurt anyone else!"

Dexter pulled a branch down a little so it hid his face.

"Mr. Wiseman wasn't that mean," he said finally. "I mean, he didn't do anything he should get *fired* for."

"What did he do?" Robin asked.

Dexter stayed quiet. He kind of hoped that if he stayed quiet long enough, Robin would get bored and wander off. But he peeked out of the leaves, and Robin was still there.

"He just, uh, he . . ." Dexter mumbled.

"What?" Robin demanded.

"He asked me where my parents were."

Dexter was whispering now. He hoped Robin hadn't heard him.

But then Robin said, "That's *it*? That's all he did?"

Dexter shrugged.

"Did he say it in a really mean way, like—" Robin hunched up his shoulders and made his voice deep and scary-sounding. "'Where are your parents, young man? That's right! I'm talking to you! Where are your parents?'"

"No," Dexter admitted. "He didn't say it like that."

"Then how was he mean?"

Dexter closed his eyes, and it was like he was back in the school office, that first day. He was standing in front of the counter, barely able to see over.

"Um—hello?" he said, but none of the adults behind the counter heard him. He saw the secretary make a bad face and clutch her stomach for a minute. Then the phone rang and she answered it.

"Oh, Ethan and Emma are both sick today? What a shame . . . Yes, there is a lot of that going around. . . ."

I'm invisible, Dexter thought. *I could stand here for hours and nobody would notice. Nobody would care.*

Then a deep voice had boomed overhead. "You don't need a pass to get into class," the voice said. "The first bell hasn't rung yet. Just go on to your classroom and you'll be fine."

Dexter looked up at the biggest man he'd ever seen in his life. The man was leaning down toward Dexter, like a giant in a fairy tale. A name tag dangled from a string around the man's neck: "Jonathan Wiseman, Principal."

"I'm new," Dexter said. "I don't know where my classroom is."

"Oh." The principal looked around, a puzzled squint on his face. "Where are your parents? They need to come in to register you. . . ."

After that, Dexter's memory got fuzzy. It seemed like he stood there for hours, his face burning, his eyes prickling, his ears ringing with those words, "Where are your parents?" Those words made him feel like an orphan; they made him feel like a kid that nobody loved.

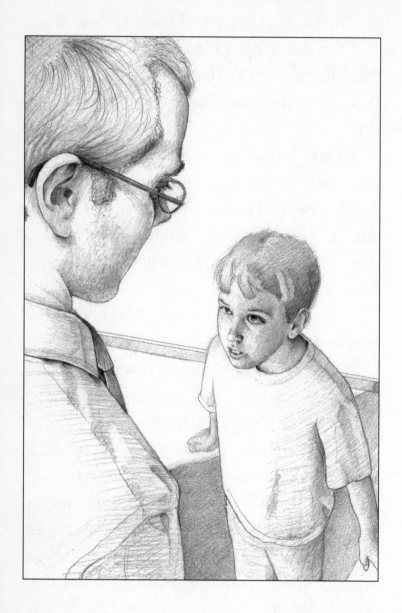

But maybe it was only a few minutes before the secretary walked over and said, "Oh, this is Dexter Jackson. His grandmother stopped in to register him last week. Her work schedule prevented her from coming in this morning, and she wanted to make sure . . ."

Blah, blah, blah, blah, blah. The only words that mattered were the cruel ones: *Where are your parents?*

Now he told Robin stiffly, "You wouldn't understand."

"But . . . then . . . do you want to go talk to the secretary? Remember, Mr. Chandler says she makes really good chocolate chip cookies, and—"

"No."

"Do you want to go help Mr. Chandler test out new floor wax?"

"Robin, that is so stupid! Just leave me alone! Just go away, okay?"

Dexter's voice sounded every bit as mean as the pretend-principal voice Robin had imitated.

On the other side of the branch, Robin's face was getting blurry. Dexter pulled the branch down all the way in front of him, so it hid him completely.

When he looked out again, Robin was gone.

Chapter 18

Dear Ms. Abbott,

You know how you said I should do something else,
not write about a fight? And I said I wanted to write
about a fight? I changed my mind. I don't want to
write about a fight anymore. I'll write about anything
you want me to write about. Just not that fight.

Sinserly,

Dexter Jackson

Dexter clutched his paper as he walked to
Ms. Abbott's desk. He hoped she'd count a
letter as his next writing assignment.

But Ms. Abbott's eyes narrowed as she read
the letter. She tapped her finger on her chin.

"Dexter?" she said gently. "Why did you change your mind?"

"I don't know," Dexter said. "I just did."

Ms. Abbott raised one eyebrow.

"Hmm. We have a problem, then," she said. "Because I changed my mind too."

"You did?" Dexter said. Suddenly he had a sinking feeling in the pit of his stomach.

"Yes," Ms. Abbott said. "Now I think you *need* to write about that fight."

That wasn't fair. Teachers weren't supposed to change their minds. They were supposed to know everything. They were supposed to make a decision and stick with it.

"Why?" Dexter asked.

Ms. Abbott toyed with one strand of her hair. She wrapped it around her finger, then let it spring free.

"I have a theory," she said.

"What?" Dexter blurted out.

"I think this fight really happened," Ms. Abbott said. "And what you've written"— she ruffled through the papers in Dexter's file—"I think it's all true. Except for the part where you said the fight didn't matter."

That did it. Now the pit of Dexter's stomach felt like it had sunk all the way down to his tennis shoes.

"But I said it wasn't true!" Dexter protested. "*Robin* told you it never happened!"

She gave him a strange look. Oops. Now she'd know he eavesdropped.

"I admit, I'm a little confused," she said. "Why would both of you lie? And if you beat Robin up, why would Robin's teacher say that he seems to be adjusting so much better—and seems so much happier—since the two of you started playing together?"

Great. Now Robin's teacher knew about the fight, too.

"We don't *play*," Dexter said. "See, I just had a lot of bad things happen to me that first day. And—"

"I'm sorry to hear that," Ms. Abbott said. Dexter shrugged.

"It doesn't matter now," he said. "But Robin wants to hunt down everyone who was mean to me. *He* thinks everybody's really nice, and they're going to apologize, or something."

Ms. Abbott smiled.

"He sounds like a good friend," she said.

"He's not my friend!" Dexter protested. "I beat him up, okay?"

Ms. Abbott just looked at him. Now she had both eyebrows raised.

Dexter realized what he'd done.

"You tricked me!" he complained. "You made me confess!"

Ms. Abbott smoothed out his paper.

"You confessed in writing a long time ago," she said. "And nobody made you do that."

Dexter slumped in his chair. He remembered how he'd felt that first day, pressing his pencil down on the paper, spelling out I am tuf. It was like he'd been some entirely other person.

"It felt like I had to," Dexter said. "Like I'd explode if I didn't get the words out."

"I'm glad you didn't explode," Ms. Abbott said gently. "And I'm glad you didn't turn out to be the kind of kid who gets into lots of fights, all the time. That first day, I didn't know that your dad was sick, or that your mother was away with him. I didn't know why you were staying with your grand-mother . . . you've certainly had a lot to deal with, haven't you?"

Ms. Abbott didn't even know about the principal being mean, and the secretary aban-doning him, and the kids laughing about him. She didn't know all the reasons he'd been so mad he *had* to hit Robin.

Except—it turned out that none of those things were as bad as he'd thought.

And, anyhow, none of them were Robin's fault.

Dexter stared down at his paper. His face felt like it was burning up again.

"I'm kind of surprised that you didn't

want to write about your family's situation," Ms. Abbott said. "Sometimes writing like that can be very therapeutic."

Dexter's face got hotter. She didn't understand. Some things he would never write about. Some words and feelings were stuck deep, deep inside him.

"Dexter?" Ms. Abbott said. "Do you think there's a connection between what was going on in your family, and the fight you had with Robin?"

Dexter thought about his father lying in his hospital bed, not moving. He thought about his hand hitting Robin's face. He shook his head.

"Sometimes bad things happen to good people," he said. This was something his mom had told him, when his dad first got sick. "Sometimes lots of bad things happen." He thought about how he'd felt that first day, with his father sick, his mother gone, his grandmother unable to get off work to bring him to school. When the secretary left him and the big kids laughed at him, he felt like he was caught in an avalanche of bad things.

He swallowed hard and kept talking.

"The bad things that happened to me—they just happened," he said. "They weren't my fault. But me hitting Robin—I did that. I was the bad one."

The words on his paper swam before his eyes. He waited for Ms. Abbott to tell him what his punishment was. Maybe he'd have to go to the principal's office. Maybe he'd be kicked out of school. Probably she'd have to call Grandma and Mom and Dad. That would be the worst thing of all.

But then he felt Ms. Abbott patting his back.

"Maybe I'm missing something," Ms. Abbott said. "But it seems like Robin's forgiven you."

She really didn't understand. That just made it worse, the fact that Robin was nice to him.

"The question is," Ms. Abbott added, "what do you have to do to forgive yourself?"

Dexter kept his head down. But he dared to peek over sideways at Ms. Abbott.

"Aren't you going to punish me?" he asked.

"No," Ms. Abbott said. "But—" She gathered up Dexter's papers and slipped them into his hands. "Keep writing about the fight."

Chapter 19

Robin was back in the grass at recess. Once again, he was tearing up blades of grass and dropping them on the ground. Dexter paced around the playground, watching. He told himself there were plenty of other things he could do—maybe he should join the kickball game, after all. But he kept circling back toward Robin. His third time around, he finally walked right over to him.

Robin barely glanced up.

"Hey," Dexter said.

"Hey," Robin said. He tore another blade of grass in half.

Dexter sat down.

"I thought you were helping the janitor," he said.

Robin shrugged.

"It's no fun alone," he said.

Dexter thought about pointing out that if Robin was helping the janitor, he wouldn't be alone. He'd be with the janitor. But Dexter knew what Robin meant. Robin wouldn't have fun helping the janitor without Dexter helping, too.

Robin peeled three more blades of grass down to their veins.

Dexter picked up one of the grass pieces Robin dropped.

"I bet nobody could ever glue this back together," he said. "Not even with superglue."

"I guess not," Robin said. But he stopped tearing up blades of grass and started watching Dexter.

Dexter lined up the ripped pieces of grass on a bare patch of ground. He made a pattern: short, long, short, long. He curved the line of grass into a curlicue.

"Ever done something you wanted to take back?" he asked Robin.

"Sure," Robin said.

"Like what?" Dexter asked, still moving grass strips around.

"Well . . . one time I fed my dog a Hershey's bar," Robin said. "Mom told me a million times that Petunia can't have people food, but I just thought, everybody loves chocolate. It's mean not to give Petunia some. So I did."

"What happened?" Dexter asked.

"Petunia got really, really sick," Robin said.

"And you wanted to take back the chocolate, but you couldn't, because it was too late?" Dexter said.

Robin frowned at him.

"Sort of. But Petunia got so sick that she threw everything up, so it was kind of like she did give the candy back."

Dexter made a disgusted face.

"Yuck," he said.

"Yeah, it was really gross," Robin said. But he sounded happy about it.

Dexter had run out of grass pieces. He hadn't put any grass blades back together, but he'd made a cool design.

"I want to take something back, too," Dexter said. "Something I can't change at all."

"What?" Robin said.

"I'm sorry I beat you up," Dexter said, the words coming out in a rush.

Robin squinted at him, puzzled.

"What do you mean?" he said. "You never beat me up."

"Huh?" Dexter said, letting out such a great huff of air that he scattered all the loose pieces of grass. "What are you talking about? Of course I beat you up! Remember? In the bathroom? When you were crying? My first day at school?"

"That? That wasn't beating me up," Robin said.

"Yes it was!" Dexter had never expected to have to fight about whether or not they'd had a fight. "I hit you all those times, you didn't hit back—I won!"

Robin stared at him, his jaw dropped.

"Dexter, you only hit me once," he said.

"That's crazy!" Dexter said. "I hit you with my fist, and then—"

He tried to remember. He could see his fist crashing into Robin's jaw. He'd played that scene in his mind so many times. But what had happened next?

"You yelled at me," Robin said. "You screamed, 'Stop crying! Don't ever cry! Don't let anyone see you cry!'"

Dexter remembered that. He remembered how much he'd wanted to cry, how close he'd come to letting the tears out, even as he yelled at Robin. He remembered why he was so mad at Robin: Because Robin was crying, and Dexter couldn't.

"And then," Robin said, "you just stared at me for a few minutes, like you were waiting for me to stop crying. And then you ran out of the bathroom again."

Dexter blinked. Robin was right. That was what had happened. Dexter remembered skidding out of the bathroom, and seeing the secretary again. She'd still looked pale, with sweat beads on her lip. And then she'd taken him on to Ms. Abbott's class. That was how everything had happened. But the way Robin told the story, so calmly—that wasn't how it had felt. Dexter had felt crazy, like someone turning into a monster in a comic book. Dexter felt like he'd hit Robin a million times. He *felt* like he'd beat him up.

"Well, anyway," Dexter said, a little sheepishly. "I did hit you. Why didn't you tell on me? Why didn't you tattle? Right then—that morning? Why didn't you run down to the office and say, 'Hey! The new kid just punched me! Look! I have bruises!'?"

"I don't know," Robin said, shrugging. He picked up a handful of grass pieces, and let them sift back down to the ground. "I guess because . . . all the other kids were trying to get me to cry, you know? When they called me crybaby—they were happy when that made me cry harder. It gave them more to laugh at. But you . . . you didn't want me to cry. It kind of seemed like you were trying to help."

"That's crazy," Dexter said. "I hit you."

It was sad that so many kids had been mean to Robin, that he thought someone who hit him was actually being nice.

Then Dexter remembered something else.

"But you told your mom," he said.

"No, I didn't," Robin said.

"Yes, you *did*," Dexter said. "I heard you, at the park, just as Grandma was driving me away. You said, 'See, Mom, that's the boy I was telling you about, the one who beat me up.' Or, 'hit me.' Or something like that."

Robin shook his head.

"You're wrong," he said. "What I said was, 'See, Mom, that's the boy I was telling you about. The one who said "Bryce" was a good last name. The one who . . .'" Robin looked down at the grass, avoiding Dexter's eyes. "'The one who's going to be my friend.'"

Dexter didn't say anything.

Robin looked back up, a little wild-eyed.

"It's true!" he said. "Don't you know what my mom would have done if I said you hit me? She would have talked to the principal. She would have called your parents. She would have taken me out of school. She would have been really, really mad!"

Dexter believed him.

"I am sorry," Dexter said.

Robin nodded.

"I know."

The two of them sat in the grass for a long time. Dexter thought about what a strange kid Robin was. Dexter never would have talked like this with any of his friends back home. Of course, he also hadn't been able to talk to his friends back home about his dad being sick. And they *knew* about Dexter's dad—their moms must have told them. Dexter knew they knew because they gave him strange looks sometimes, and Jaydell and Dillon wouldn't play at Dexter's house anymore. "No, sorry, I've got to go home and do . . . chores,"

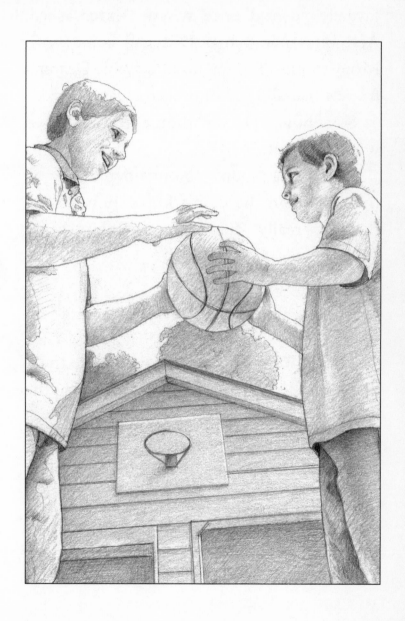

Jaydell had said once when Dexter asked. And one time when Dad had come with Mom to pick Dexter up at school, Dexter's friends had all kind of backed away, scared.

Somehow, Dexter didn't think Robin would do that.

But Dexter didn't know how to say all that to Robin; he didn't know how to say that he really didn't mind Robin being strange.

And then he did.

"Hey, Robin?" he said. "Want to shoot some hoops?"

Robin looked up, startled. And then, watching Robin's face was like watching the sun rise. Robin knew Dexter wasn't just asking about basketball.

"Yeah," Robin said, his face glowing. "I sure do."

Chapter 20

Sometimes true stories have more than one story in them. I was really mad when I hit Robin that first day at school. I was mad at everybody. I was even mad at my dad, and all he did was get sick. (But he's going to get better now.)

So I was mad at everybody, but the person I hit was Robin. Because he was there. And he was crying, and that's what I wanted to do too, only I'm not a crybaby. (And he isn't either, now.)

And after I hit Robin, and I wasn't so mad anymore, I felt really bad about it. It was all I could think about, which made me feel worse, because I should have been thinking about my dad and not being any trouble for Grandma.

But the other stories in my story are other people's stories. I thought the secreterry and the prinsipel and the janiter were trying to be mean to me, but they weren't. And even though I was being mean to Robin, he thought I was trying to be his friend. And now I am, so I guess Robin was right after all.

Dexter sat back in his chair at Grandma's table. It was late—he could hear Grandma snoring in the living room. Mixed with the sound of the man on TV, her snores actually sounded like harmony.

Dexter read his story one more time. It had taken him so long to write—it was probably the longest thing he'd ever written in his whole life. Probably Ms. Abbott would find lots of things she'd still want him to change. But Dexter was happy with it.

He was happy, too, because he was going to go home from school with Robin tomorrow. Robin had said they could play with Petunia and ride bikes in the park. Robin's parents had even fixed up Dexter's bike, so it would work better now.

And Mom and Dad had called last night to say that Dad should be out of the hospital by the end of December. He'd still have to stay in Seattle for a few more months after that, but they were hoping that Dexter and Grandma could come out and visit during Dexter's Christmas break.

Maybe they'd even get to go up in the Space Needle—all of them. All together.

Dexter looked down at his story and thought of one more sentence. Even though his hand ached from writing so much, he gripped his pencil and added, very carefully:

I don't feel like hitting anyone anymore.